Set: 1

One Hundred Is a Family

One Hundred Is a Family

Pam Muñoz Ryan

Illustrated by Benrei Huang

Hyperion Paperbacks for Children
New York

First Hyperion Paperback edition 1996

Text ©1994 by Pam Muñoz Ryan.
Illustrations © 1994 by Benrei Huang.

A hardcover edition of *One Hundred Is a Family* is available from Hyperion Books for Children.

Printed in the United States of America.

1 3 5 7 9 10 8 6 4 2

Library of Congress Cataloging-in-Publication Data
Ryan, Pam Muñoz
One hundred is a family / by Pam Muñoz Ryan—
1st ed.
p.   cm.
Summary: Groups making up many different kinds of
"families" introduce the numbers from one to ten and
then by tens to one hundred.
ISBN 1-56282-672-7 (trade)
ISBN 1-56282-673-5 (lib. bdg.)—ISBN 0-7868-1120-X (pbk.)
[1. Family—Fiction.
2. Family life—Fiction. 3. Counting.
4. Stories in rhyme.] I. Title
II. Title: 100 is a family.
PZ8.3.R955On   1994
[E]—dc20   93-30914

The artwork for this book is prepared using watercolor and ink.
The text for this book is set in 18-point Slimbach.

To my children's teachers:
Cathy Bullock, Debra Du Chateau,
Darice Fenton, Ruth Johnson,
Judy Leff, Mary Lou Schultz, and Bea Wood
—P.M.R.

To Barbara, P.K., and Emily
and the families they cherish
—B.H.

ONE is a family
finding
a place to call home.

TWO is a family
starting
a new life of their own.

THREE is a family
counting
the sparkling stars at night.

FOUR is a family
waking
to morning's first light.

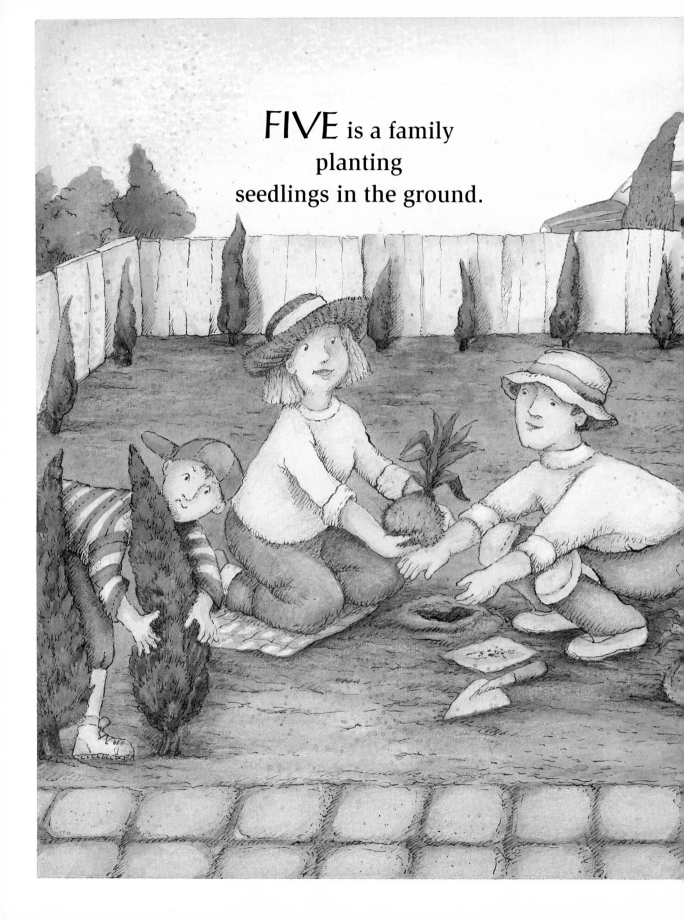

FIVE is a family
planting
seedlings in the ground.

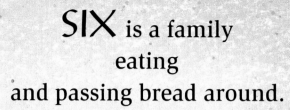

SIX is a family
eating
and passing bread around.

SEVEN is a family
keeping
traditions of the past.

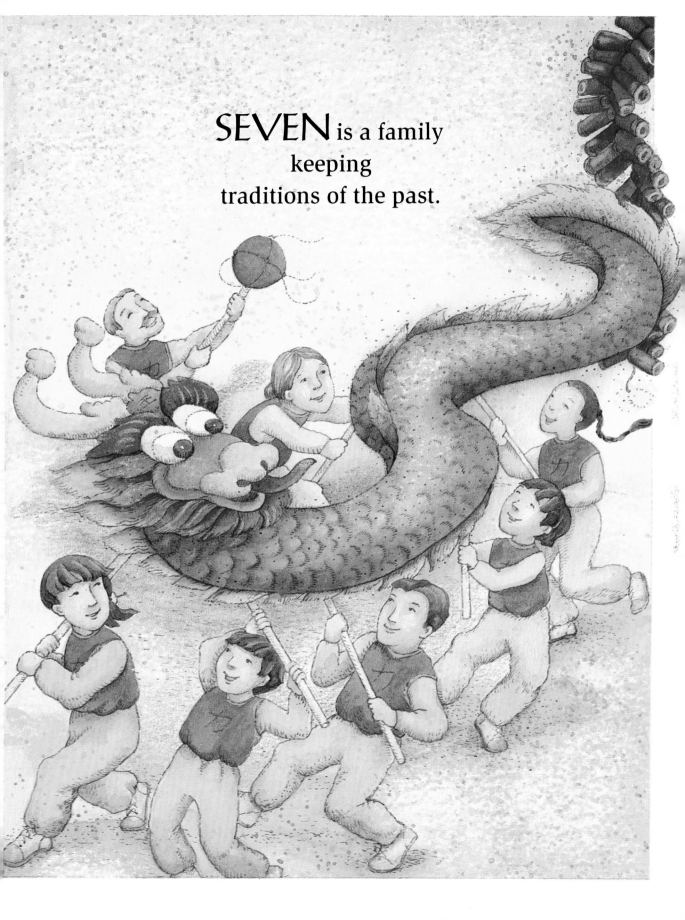

EIGHT is a family
quilting
strong stitches that last.

NINE is a family
remembering
other times and places.

TEN is a family
cheering
runners round the bases.

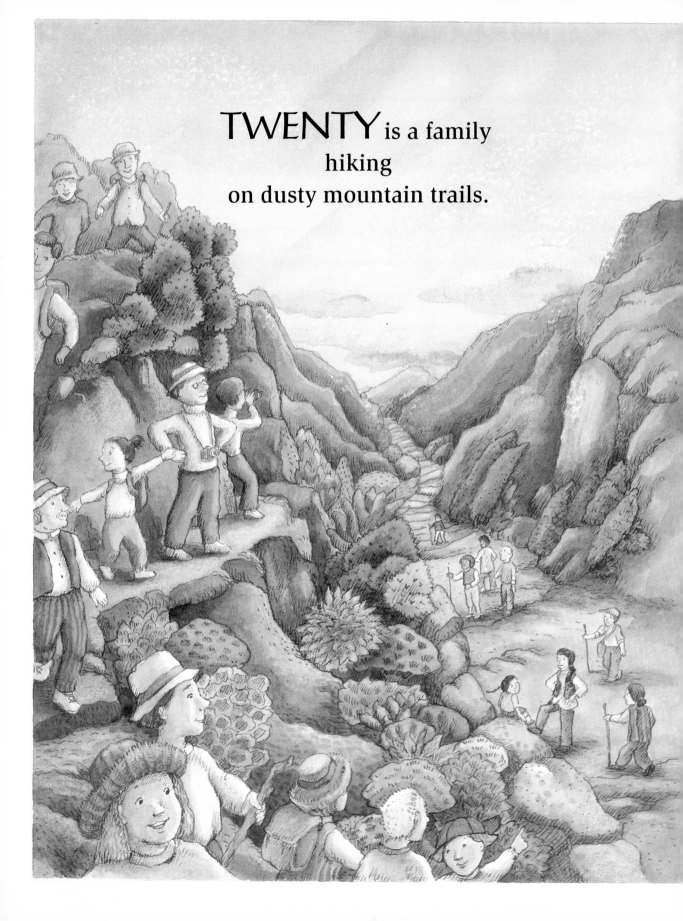

TWENTY is a family
hiking
on dusty mountain trails.

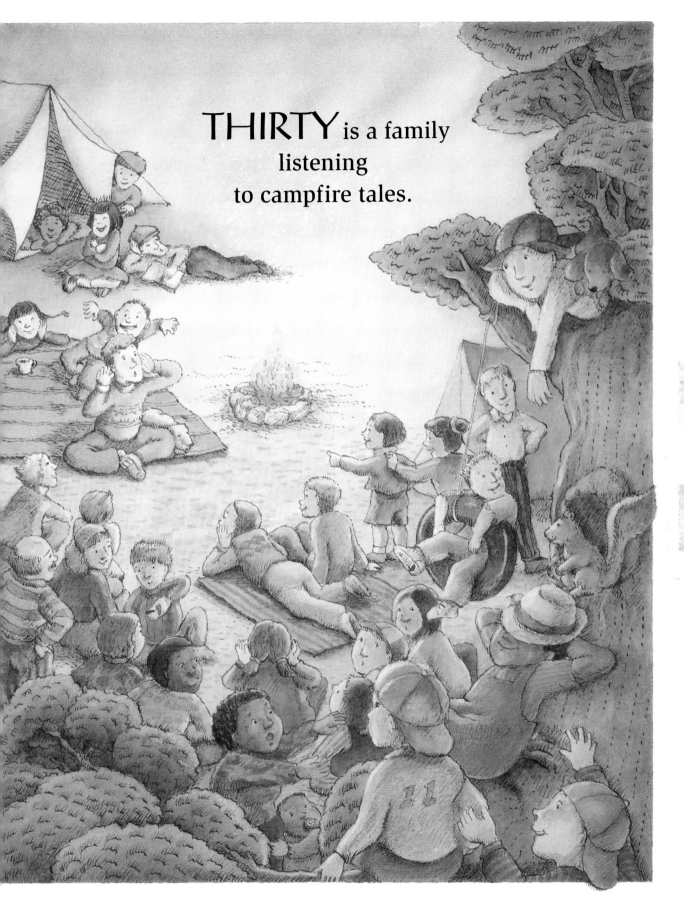

THIRTY is a family
listening
to campfire tales.

FORTY is a family
bringing
the ripened harvest in.

FIFTY is a family
mending
after an angry wind.

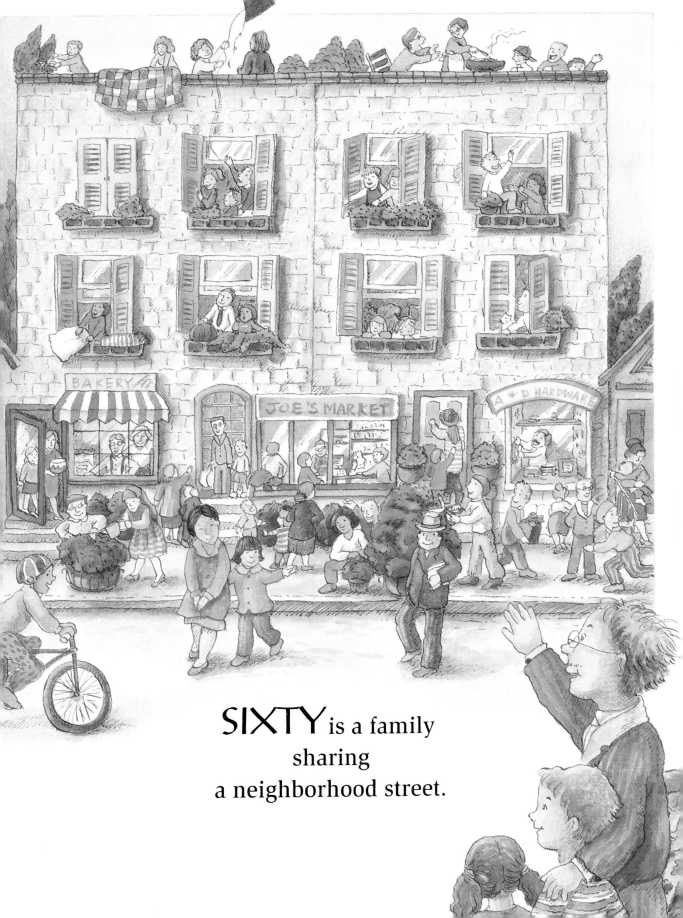

SIXTY is a family
sharing
a neighborhood street.

SEVENTY is a family
fixing
a festive place to meet.

EIGHTY is a family
singing
a round of joyful songs.

NINETY is a family
knowing
they all belong.

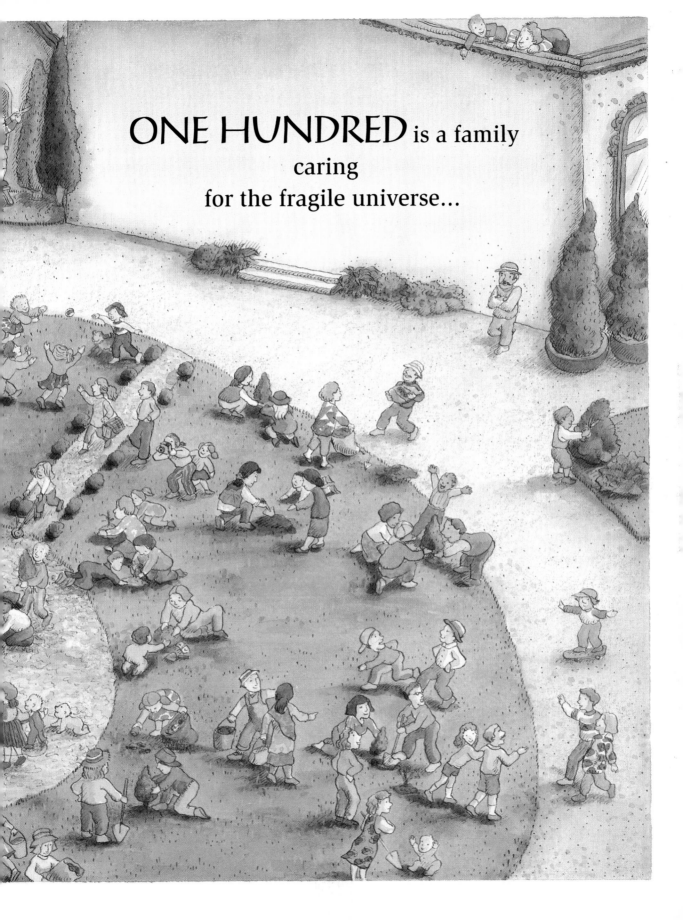

ONE HUNDRED is a family
caring
for the fragile universe...

and making life
better
for every ONE on earth.